Butterfly Rising

Romance Wealth Series, Volume 5

Ava Axton

Published by Ava Axton, 2023.

BUTTERFLY RISING

First edition. May 17, 2023.

ISBN: 979-8223052241

Written by Ava Axton.

Also by Ava Axton

Romance Wealth Series
Butterfly Rising

Watch for more at https://www.amazon.com/author/avaaxton.

Table of Contents

Dedication

To the women of yore, who lived as concubines.......

Your stories have been overlooked and forgotten for too long. You endured challenges that many cannot even begin to imagine, and yet you persevered. You navigated the treacherous waters of court politics and battled against a society that viewed you as property rather than as individuals.

You faced the constant fear of being cast aside, replaced by a younger, more desirable woman. You were forced to live in the shadows, unable to fully express yourselves or your desires. You bore children who would never be fully recognized by society and who would forever carry the label of "illegitimate."

And yet, you found ways to survive. You formed alliances with other women in the same position, providing each other with support and companionship. You honed your skills in music, art, and literature, becoming experts in the very fields that your society deemed frivolous.

Through your strength and resilience, you paved the way for future generations of women. You showed us that even in the darkest of times, there is still hope. That we can still find joy and love and beauty in a world that seeks to diminish us.

So to the women of yore who lived as concubines, this dedication is for you.

May your stories be remembered and your legacies live on.

BUTTERFLY RISING

By
Ava Axton

<u>INTRODUCTION</u>

An engaging fictionalized account of the 16th century King of England, Henry VIII's romance with Anne Boleyn dubbed "the King's great matter". It explores the events of the life and death of the infamous Anne Boleyn and the passion and tragedy brought by her marriage to King Henry VIII.

Anne's blood had long dried. That of the King too.

This is set after the demise of the King, during the rule of his desired heir - Edward VI, a story of the end of his unpropitious reign after which Catherine's daughter, Mary becomes the Queen of England. Fierce and blood thirstier than her father, she has scars from memories of Anne Boleyn. Catherine harbors great contempt for Anne's daughter - Elizabeth.

Follow Elizabeth - stunning, smart, vindictive - her mother's daughter as she grows up in a world of enemies seeking pounds of her flesh as retribution for her mother's "sins". She steadily learns the act of thriving with subtlety and patience. She perfects this game - this long game of chess she has been playing since her mother's death. This game she plans to win.

Both the scariest and most beautiful thing there is. We witness a butterfly burst gloriously out of its cocoon and shimmer so brightly.

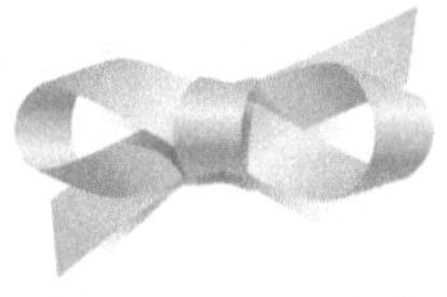

CHAPTER 1

P*ROLOGUE*
   England 1547

The King's burial has long been done with, the mourning period a distant memory.

A boy with a full head of blonde curls walked in the center of the standing congregation, through their stares, up the dais and stood with his elder sisters, discarded from succession in favor of him. The boy stood proud, assured, and swore his oaths to God and man - to protect and serve the people of England! Cheers rented the air as he sat on the throne. King Edward VI, successor, ruler. What a task for a nine-year-old.

Elizabeth walked up the dais, her stepsister's arm looped tensely through hers. They both sat in their chairs - a level lower than their brother's - a message and one she understood. She smiled up at Edward and at her sister who dropped her hand.

The court buzzed merrily, commoners, nobles, together to celebrate the new King. Princess Elizabeth sunk deeper into her seat, she was young enough to slouch and cause no scandal. She was bored and angry. She smiled and wilted and smiled some more, over, and over through the hours it took for the celebration to end.

As she had suspected, Edward, ever suspicious and cautious, declared that Elizabeth would return with her stepmother -

Catherine Parr. She would learn from her what only a mother could teach.

Soon, Catherine wed Thomas Seymour, brother to the woman that had killed her mother. They all moved in together, the Seymour's and Elizabeth. None of her pleas had changed Edward's decision. The Princess resolved to be strong.

PRINCESS ELIZABETH
Chelsea England 1547

Elizabeth was startled awake in her own bed by a roaming hand up her thigh and knew there would be no more sleep for the night.

There had not been for the past months. A familiar musk caged her. She knew without looking that he had come visiting again.

"What do you seek again?"

"Be that anyway to greet your father?" Thomas Seymour laughed.

"A father doesn't sneak into his daughter's room to caress her!" She yelled, jumping out of her sheets to unlock her door. Unyielding, it remained locked.

"I just want to play." He teased, shaking the keys, their crinkling echoing through the room.

A sob rose from within Elizabeth as she crumpled onto the floor. She did not want to play and started screaming. She wailed so loud the entire household heard her and came to her rescue.

Poundings echoed against the bedroom's door, inquiries, and yelling. Elizabeth now stood flush against the door and heard the man come close. He leaned down and dug his nose into the expanse of skin on her neck while his hand came up to grab her breast. "Soo intoxicating." Her heartbeat, loud thunder in her head.

Then, in a flash, Thomas Seymour pulled her behind him and unlocked the door, a charming smile on his face. Outside the door they stared into the brightness of the hall lights, his wife and the staff looking on.

Quickly, Thomas wove a tale of how she had suffered a nightmare. That she had mistook his petting hands for the monsters of her dream. His wife sighed and praised his kindness and lauded him with a kiss on the cheek. She then hurried over to embrace Elizabeth, tight, almost painful.

And soon they all sought to leave the Princess insisted on a maid. She insisted and Thomas could do nothing but acquiesce, commenting on the fears of a child.

That night under the watchful gaze of a maid, she managed to sleep better.

She woke to the brightness of the sunlight in her room. Her head was pounding as she recalled the affairs of the previous night. The maid - Jane, was now sleeping pressed against her. Her hand was tossed firmly around her. Jane's nose nestled in Elizabeth's ear. She wondered if Jane could sense the illness too. The illness of Thomas Seymour's actions. She wondered if the entire household did. She was torn between rage and fear and wished that the staff could do more but could not blame them. Not when her stepmother - Catherine Parr was a blind supporter of her husband's rotten twisted games, blindly in love with him. Not even her brother, the King believed her letters.

She wished for a soul-friend, the only candidate her mother, now long gone. Elizabeth put a hand against her chest and clasped the locket that dangled from her neck - her mother's locket. She accepted the comfort and strength it brought her. Elizabeth let her hand drop back to her mattress.

Princess Elizabeth got out of bed that day and wrote a letter to her brother. She demanded her right as a Princess - a bevy of maids-of-honor. The King could not deny her.

The Princess grew in her studies, under the watchful eye of her guardians and maids. She blossomed.

• • ❧ • •

T*HOMAS SEYMOUR*
England 1548

Thomas could only fume and dance to the tune under the indignity Elizabeth had chosen for him to suffer.

Once she received her precious maids, she made sure to never be alone without them. She even insisted on having her own guards. Their loyalty was like steel, fulfilling her every wish.

Too many people surrounded Elizabeth now. Gone where the opportunities to run his hand over the growing curves of her body in the guise of tickling. His devious attempts to sneak into her bed to caress her breasts at night, were no more. She would not even pay him a glance. She planned to travel soon, uncaring about his affections. Damn her! He had plans for her. O the things he could have helped her achieve.

His mouth was parched, his tongue leaden in his mouth. What he would not give for a caress of her dark waves to ease a bit of the roaring in his veins. A kiss perhaps? That would settle the painful throbbing in his groin.

These days he found himself taking Catherine to bed more often, more roughly. All his warmth and glee focused on thoughts of his stepdaughter. Catherine was not suspicious yet.

She was oblivious to the fact that his moans during their lovemaking were not for her, rather for Elizabeth. His body had betrayed him, his mind, and thoughts too. He did not care. He loved it this way, this almost pervasive love he felt.

He knew straying from his subtle advances would only ensure that she would run permanently away. That is, if the young King did not take his head. He had to be more patient. Much more.

One day he would find her, delightfully unguarded and willing. He would bind her in great manacles, both on her wrists and ankles. This would ensure they were well anchored into the stone floor and walls, firm but not bruising. He planned to cut the dress off her delicate frame and tease her with damning words. He would touch her, lick her, and prod her; on and on. Then she would break, scream, and beg him to take her. And take her he would. Her body first, then her mind and through her he would have his needs satiated – physically and politically.

Soon he hoped.

Soon................

The door groaned open, and a woman stepped through the threshold, a wide smile on her beautiful face. Her under garment was dark and embroidered with golden thread and her skin glistened under the reflection of the full moon's filter. If he was startled by her entrance, he did not reveal it.

Catherine Parr - his wife.

He sat up and watched as she strutted into the room, her eyes on him the entire time. She stopped at the foot of the bed and stood watching him, her eyes blazing with need. "It is a cold night My lord," she said. "I hope to please you."

He grinned up at her, reaching his hand out to take hers, grateful for the opportunity to imagine her as Elizabeth.

Quickly, he pulled her sharply, holding her tightly against him as their lips locked in an embrace far from every semblance of propriety, greed, and need. When they broke apart, her face was flushed, her eyes shining. Her breathing - erratic. "What do you have in mind......My Lady."

Quietly, Catherine reached for him again, putting her warm hand on the back of his neck. She lifted his lips to hers. They kissed, first lightly, then more urgently, his tongue in her mouth. Ardently, her hips flushed against his, her breasts pressing firmly against his chest. He flipped her over suddenly, eager to lose himself inside his imagination of her being Elizabeth. He planned to sheath himself completely in her.

She pulled away, laughing, and slipped down the bed. She unfastened his pants and eased them over his hips. She lightly brushed past the length of his throbbing member with her palm before taking him in her mouth. He sighed, eyes shut, thinking about how unbelievably good it felt. How experienced she was. Surely, he had to teach Elizabeth this.

He looked down and her eyes were locked on his, as she opened her mouth. She hollowed her cheeks, and slid his girth, all the way down. He groaned and found himself pumping into her mouth. The slick sound of saliva echoing in the dim lighted room.

He pulled her up, left her under garment on and laid her on her side before laying behind her. He tossed her leg over his thigh until she was wide open and eager to receive him. He slipped his finger into her warm depths. "Elizabeth," he whispered. He listened to her forget herself, screaming in pleasure, as he twisted his fingers within her quim.

Thomas felt her squeeze and clamp her thighs against his wrist. She twisted her hips, once, twice, three times and then froze. All the muscles in her thighs and belly tensed and quivered, and he felt her contract against his fingers.

Before she could recover, he rolled her onto her back and slipped inside her. After the first few thrusts, he had to hold still, knowing that if he kept moving, he would explode. He paced himself in tempo to the exquisite firmness, and the heat, lest he lose control. He wanted to draw this out. He wanted to extend her pleasure, like he planned for Elizabeth.

Gradually, he built up the teasing, until he could no longer wait. He sped up, slamming deeper into her, her screams echoing through the room and beyond. Now he was seeing stars and was crumbling apart. His world was ecstasy! With a guttural roaring he delighted in claiming his wife again, and repeatedly. Elizabeth was the only image in his mind.

CHAPTER 2

Princess Elizabeth
Chelsea England 1548

The Princess walked the muddy pathway of the Manor's gardens. It has rained recently. She delighted herself in the quietness, save for the chirping of birds. She enjoyed the protection the shade of the trees provided alongside the guards on sentry for her beckoning.

In the few months that had passed, Elizabeth had acquired an astonishing amount of awareness and a cautious nature, far above her tender age of fourteen.

Her trusted allies were her maids, tutors, and Governess - Mistress Catherine Ashley. Elizabeth was so fond of her that she called her Mistress Kat. Kat felt the same way too, for she allowed informality.

Lord Thomas's behavior towards her had taken a steady decline, now deemed merely courteous. He sought opportunities to have her alone. Shameless in his pursuit, Elizabeth's Stepmother now aided him. Her blindness to his apparent "plays" appalling.

She had held Elizabeth down and muffled her mouth while her husband tore her gown into shreds. She had laughed while he roamed his hands over her body, a violation Catherine deemed fatherly. Twice, that had happened. On the third time, Elizabeth had hidden a butterknife in her bodice and had bled them enough to escape.

Yet no one believed her tales, not Edward, nor Mary, not even Cat and her maids-of-honor. They did not feel inclined to believe a word from the mouth of Anne Boleyn's daughter.

So, Elizabeth had decided to never let the opportunity of her seclusion with either of her molesters. If anything, she buried herself in her studies and charity, on the opportunities she was free.

Kat told her about her mother and how she loved Charity. She told of how she gave as often as she could, despite being busy she as Queen, and even before she had wed.

Elizabeth did not remember much of her mother. She remembered the warmth her presence used to give. She remembered the memory of her smile. Surely, she remembered her death. It was impossible not to. Now, every smile Mary sent her was filled with smugness.

Life as a Princess was lavish and excessive. She could give to Charity and Kat had deemed her lucky enough to have her brother's care, as little as he did. It was a fact Elizabeth needed no reminder of. A tough pill she had long swallowed. More than anything Elizabeth wanted to leave England, travel like her mother had to France, to learn an enticing culture, to escape Thomas.

Elizabeth trailed the muddy pathways, humming quietly as she twisted through the trees and hedges. The scent of the flowers was a welcome delight that had her smiling, almost heady.

She walked out of the garden, aware of the sentries that followed her in a distance. The terrain had shifted: to the solid cobblestoned yard that led to the Manor's entrance. The stones crunched beneath her boots, and songbirds cried overhead. Elizabeth smiled as a chill embraced her, scented with an enticing freshness that cloyed the air after rainfall.

It was not until the guards halted beyond her Chamber's doors that she noticed the silence in the Manor. She thought nothing of it.

Ever since Lady Catherine's pregnancy announcement, she needed all the hands she could get, on her trips to her routine riverside picnics. Today, Elizabeth had given her maids free reign for the day.

She nodded to her guards, comforted by the fact that they stood outside the door. She went past her unpleasant hosting room, one that her stepmother had delightedly chosen colors and into her bedroom.

Just as the Princess took off her overcoat, she sensed she was not alone. "I have been waiting for you all day."

She gasped, an icy, invisible hand quickly wrapped around her throat, making it difficult to breath. She had not considered the possibility, the possibility of him being here. "What?" She managed, moving backwards towards the door, hoping that he did not notice.

Lord Thomas Seymour stalked off her bed, tossing the chemise that he had been sniffing, an ever-gleeful smile on his face. "Haven't you toyed with me enough? Don't you care for my injured ego?"

"Stay away from me." She did not think he would do anything, yet that did not stop her from pressing her back against the door. Slowly, she lifted her hand to clasp the handle.

He laughed, mockingly and in a flash had her pressed against the door. A strong hand caged hers, a threatening knife now against her neck, "Scream, I dare you."

The maniacal gleam in his eyes terrified her. She started choking on her tears and she could only swallow as he pressed his nose into her neck. "Your scent says that you want this. Why do you keep pretending? Why?" He growled, pressing the knife against her throat, causing her to sob quietly.

She had almost forgotten how crazy he could get when they were alone. Such a strange mind he had, imagining things that were not there. "No," she wound up saying, angry at how worthlessly weak he made her feel. "I have no interest in you … pardon me."

Thomas was enraged by her response, and he froze for a moment as he stared at her. Suddenly a switch flipped, and he grabbed her and tossed her onto her bed. He dropped his knife and replaced it with his hands, choking her as he cursed in her face. He cursed and raged that she was his, even as she wheezed and gasped her pleas, he swore she would be with no one else. Her body was his, her right to the crown his to manipulate... and she gasped and shoved weakly at him. Tears spilled down her cheeks as she pleaded to God, and asked for his mercy, his right hand already deep in her thigh, when she decided to bait him.

"Wait... wait, I am willing."

"Nice try," he said, his hold on her neck now loose, his hand in her thighs halting.

She lifted a hand to his face and smiled, "Honestly, my Lord, my only fear was my stepmother, she carries your child after all."

His eyes gleamed as he smirked. "She is nobody to hinder our love, I have plans for you, my Love."

Elizabeth swallowed her disgust and held his tender gaze, "I am done pretending," she whispered.

His eyes searched for her for a quick second, and then his lips covered hers. This lunatic would kill her otherwise, and she prayed for intervention before he took it took far. Thomas took Elizabeth through the paces of her first kiss, holding her growing breast tightly. He caused her to gasp as he tangled his tongue with hers. Elizabeth's stomach churned as she tasted vomit at the back of her throat.

Fresh tears spilled anew from her eyes, her heart roaring with fear. She panicked and started pounding against his chest, but he would not let go. He started to paw at her bodice, Elizabeth bit his tongue, hard. The pandemonium drew the attention of the guards who stormed in, a flustered Catherine Parr in tow. Elizabeth bawled as she finally managed to push his shocked form off her. Clutching at her torn bodice, she rushed into a guard's arms, despaired by the accusations of reduction he swore to her stepmother.

England 1548

The biggest change in Elizabeth's imbalanced life with Seymour's finally came to a halt.

That day, a messenger from Edward had arrived. He had witnessed the affair and pregnant Catherine Parr's resulting rage.

Elizabeth had been forced to stay in her room by Kat. She had been pleading with Elizabeth not to send a letter to the King through the messenger. Her loyalty was torn between the Seymour's and Elizabeth. Elizabeth cared nothing for her pleas. She could see her pretense now, and she was done being a victim.

She hurriedly wrote a letter to King Edward, pleading for his mercy and help. She pled for a judgement through a guard

- one loyal enough to testify in her favor that travelled with the messenger.

In the weeks that followed, the Manor was wrought in tension as all waited for the King's reply. Now, Elizabeth finally felt a sense of freedom. Thomas dared not look at her, and the only ire Catherine could show was her glare.

Elizabeth's hopes had started to decline. Edward VI had counted his sister's assault of no importance. A messenger soon returned with a summons, and Elizabeth was now delighted.

That very evening she set out for the Castle, her maids, Governess, and with guards in tow.

Upon their arrival, a council was set up with King Edward as judge. Mary, Catherine, and noble council men took audience. It took many hours of talking, screaming, and witnessing. Edward's decision to grant her assaulter freedom stirred mixed feelings within her. The council departed, leaving the royal siblings alone in the room.

"My word is law," he said in an emotionless tone that made her think of their father Henry.

She stepped back, putting space between herself and the boy turned King. He had been her brother and friend while they grew up. That familiar Edward had changed so much.

Mary had offered her approval in support of Edward. Elizabeth's heart began to pound louder and faster in bewilderment. She was stunned. "You doubt my accusations?" she whispered. Unable to find any of the boldness that had helped her insist on a council, she looked at both her siblings and realized with jarring finality, they had no love for her.

"Our Stepmother's husband," Mary laughed at his side. "You could have sought attention in some other way."

A cold shudder moved down her spine. She found it impossible to remain in the room.

She stepped back, only to fall deeper into the mire of betrayal in her mind. Edward came closer, his face foreign. Her gaze moved from one sibling to the other, stopping on Edward. She found speech impossible. They had to be joking. Surely, they could not believe Thomas' demeaning statement. Surely, not over the testimonies that had been brought forth. They would condemn her to wanton, like they had her mother! "How dare you two" she managed to say seething rage finally breaking through. "How dare you!"

"It is my decision. He is free. He is banned from further contact with you," he said, his voice much quieter this time. "I do wish I could believe you." he said, raising a hand towards her.

Anger and shame heated her face as all the love she used to feel for them dried up. "You will not touch me," she hissed. Balling her hands into fists, she glared at the man in front of her. She wanted to hit him, she wanted to scream. She wanted to destroy Edward, destroy Thomas', Mary, the whole Kingdom, and every person living in it, and wipe their bigoted opinions off their faces. Only it was impossible.

"I accept then." Elizabeth said, taking in Mary's mocking smile. She turned to Edward again "I shall live with them no more, neither with you in the Castle." Despite the anger and betrayal, her voice was firm when she said, "This is wrong. You know it. I will not stay here to be degraded any further. I shall move to France and complete my studies there... please."

In her desperation, she found herself pleading with the man in front of her, begging him to assent to it.

"You may. Take all you need." he said.

Elizabeth turned to leave; her ego smitten but her spine ramrod. "I'm sorry you didn't get what you expected," Mary teased. She was telling the truth, mocking though. Right now, Mary was a perfect target to direct her anger at. Elizabeth flung words that she knew would cut deep. She wanted them to hurt Mary as much as she was hurting now.

"You can tell yourself all that you please, but it does not absolve you of the things you have done. I will be waiting, laughing, when karma decides to pay you back."

Edward and Mary visibly jerked at her words, but Mary responded. "You are facing karma's wrath, your mother's work. Do you think I fool myself? I am prepared."

Elizabeth's anger sizzled with disdain. Mary took a step back. "Learning is one of the things I excel at." Her eyes darted to King Edward who stood silently watching her. "We shall see then, in the years that come, who will have the last laugh."

Elizabeth lifted her chin, the beginning of the defiance she swore to muster. "I accept your declaration but make no mistake. It is not for fear of you. It is for me. I shall remember this, and so should you."

BUTTERFLY RISING

CHAPTER 3

P*RINCESS MARY*
England 1548

Standing at a glass hewn balcony of the Castle, Princess Mary, and her brother - King Edward VI, watched as the royal wagon was escorted out of the city. A chilly breeze swept off the grassy plains, ruffling their hair.

"France, then," Edward murmured, his dark eyes still upon the wagon. "A surprising twist of events. I thought you had planned a further ruining at Thomas' hands."

The Princess said nothing, she watched, still reeling from the last words of her stepsister.

"So do her threats bother you?"

"Obviously not," Mary said, glancing at the King. It had been on this very balcony that they had a private meeting to discuss the decision for the council.

"I plan to punish Thomas more brutally," Edward went on. "You should consider her threats."

"A child's talk brother. Hypocrisy does not befit you. You have much to learn."

Edward gave her a slow smile. "You might want to consider how you speak to me now."

"And you might want to consider whose loyalty you will never have to question."

Edward chuckled, and silent fell for a long moment. "Why did you advise it?"

Mary's attention drifted back to the wagon, already a small dot in the grassy plains beyond.

"I want her to feel the pain of being discarded by a loved one."

PRINCESS ELIZABETH

England 1548

She had been in the wagon for two hours now. Three of her maids where in a different one behind hers. She watched the moon shift and dance with the clouds. They had stopped only to pick her luggage up from Chelsea. They paused long enough for her to relieve herself and hug Kat goodbye.

She was resolute in her decision to stay in France, at least for a couple of months. There, she could pretend to be in her mother's bosom. There, she could plot and grow.

The wagon travelled farther into England and then she dozed off, falling in and out of dreams and reality.

They arrived at the port. It was surprisingly busy that night. The air was salty and fresh - a curious combination. The seagulls belted in tune with the waves and Elizabeth felt a tremor run through her. This was her first-time leaving England. She smothered the tremor and tightened her fingers. Her spine was straight as she walked up the gangplank and boarded the ship.

Princess Elizabeth knew she was nearing the docks of France, three weeks later. The endless space of water and sky gave way to gray, high rising boulders of rocks and jagged mountains that pierced the sky. She had been lying on the deck since the night before, lost in the vast beauty of the sparkling stars. Now, she could not bring herself to stand up and locate her maids, rather she stared and listened.

Sounds in the distance - shouting and gulls and revelry.

France.

She found herself quite ready for whatever France would present.

The shoreline grew clearer as they approached the docks. The ship started to blare its bells, signaling the occupants below deck of their arrival. She wished her mother were here at this moment, once again, in the country she had loved. It hurt.

She smothered a violent sob by pressing her fist to her mouth, lest it come out.

She clutched her prized locket. She would never stop missing her. A breeze filled the air, lifting away the smells of the past three weeks. Her trembling paused for a heartbeat. She loved that breeze.

She loved the sweet bite of its chill and loved the sensual essence it carried. She delighted in the fact that she would be taking temporary abode in a country whose air smelled of freedom and home.

She stood up on the deck. It was sparsely filled with eager people and her maids soon found her, luggage in hand.

She found herself sharing a smile with them, her heart full of warmth as they descended the gangplank into the city full of sounds, laughter, and spices.

Her footing was sure as she walked the graveled road to the wagon that would take her to her temporary abode.

France September 1548

The French people lived an admirable and dreamy life. Their buildings were so close to each other, unfenced and crowded.

Elizabeth thought it a miracle that chaos and clashes did not set the city ablaze. Instead, the French people were an amorously harmonious bunch. Their humor was like stone structures, twenty feet high infallible and inciting laughter.

Unlike England, the French people were much freer and more easy-going. Here, women did not have to stand so straight. The men played like infants and flirting was a social norm. They were hard workers and were well versed in the arts, music, dance, and food. Their dances were the most provocative and heady Elizabeth had ever seen. She danced, grateful for the lack of the stifling nature her English tutors had insisted. Elizabeth greedily binged on their food, both mouthwatering and ecstasy worthy.

France smelled wondrous. She could not describe it, but it was wondrous, free, accommodation. Here the streets were not all paved or cobblestoned. The houses were not all ornate or elegant. Most of the people were effortlessly stunning and their fashion sense was dizzyingly sensuous. There was a status difference in the country presented by the standard of living per individual and or household. Those who held higher positions did better and had more dresses and breeches. Nonetheless, everyone looked as if they had all there was to have in life. They smiled, they laughed, they loved, freely and openly.

The people mingled and teased with no prejudice for color or caste. The royals that had given her this privileged accommodation were delightful. They told numerous tales about her Mother Anne. They shared great tales and were honored to welcome her child.

England had shared a common tension with France since Queen Anne's death. As far as Elizabeth knew, the only thing that had caused that tension was her father's zeal to ruin everything that reminded him of her mother. Since Elizabeth had arrived, she had put an effort into assimilating with the French people - their fashion, their dance, their zeal, way of life, even their interest in reformation.

She could see how they had influenced her mother's values as a youth. In the few weeks he had been here, it had started to influence hers. Elizabeth quickly sought to have allies. These allies would be valuable against her siblings hate. Allies for a future unknown.

Her siblings had not yet sent a letter. Neither had Catherine Parr and Thomas. That was simply fine for her. She did not mind in the least. The bastards!

As if in return, she felt no inclination to do the same. they could choke on their hostility. She would prove herself worthy, work harder and excel in every aspect, no matter how hard or grey. She would not be manipulated.

Every day, Elizabeth would wake up and spend her morning and afternoon moving quickly through her tutoring for the day - Art, Sciences and Language. The French royalty had been more than eager to supply her excellent tutors. Here, unlike England, she longed to keep her eyes focused, learning and engaged. In France no longer did she have to suffer the insults and derogatory comments tossed her way about her mother. She was respected here, they loved her, and she liked it. If anything, she was sure that this adventure in France would improve her self-esteem. This experience could harm her with a bit more of the sharp tongue her mother was rumored to have.

Her boot crunched beneath her as she walked the grounds beyond the castle that evening. The air was much colder now, and snowflakes fell from the sky to accompany the awaiting pile on the ground. The carriage wheeled slowly beside her as she walked. Elizabeth had insisted on walking the entire way back. Her maids and guards had insisted she stay.

She preferred to walk on such occasions. It allowed her to observe the true face of France. People were usually out in droves by the time she reached the market. This section of the city was marked by an accessible area and was often crowded with people and kiosks. Today was no exception. If anything, the crowd was much larger than usual.

A maid hurried up to need her. She attempted to pull Elizabeth closer to her and advised that she sit inside the carriage. She did not want Elizabeth to be forced to squeeze her way through the people gathered in the center of the market.

"I wish to keep moving," Elizabeth laughed while gesturing to Mira.

Elizabeth remained unflinching, she nodded and decided to walk with her. Elizabeth laughed and teased Mira who quickly tried to move faster, elbowing a path for Elizabeth to walk through the crowd.

Mira was a shy thing, always avoiding eye contact as her only defense. Elizabeth dragged her heel and insisted that she would not be hauled around. However, she decided to bask in the attention that was thrown their way. She spent the next hour in that spot in the marketplace interacting with strangers – both friendly and kind, enjoying the delightful deed of putting smiles on their faces. Through the entire time, she spent her coins on items and quickly gave them away. She enjoyed it and soon even Mira could not resist as she joined in. Soon they had to leave, and the Princess finally climbed into the carriage. Her heart now warmed, she waved at the many strangers she had met, and off to the Castle they went.

That evening while she sat and talked with her maids, a messenger arrived in the castle. Breathless and demure, in his hand was a letter from England, from Edward.

Elizabeth's anger could not prevent the pain she felt as she read its contents - Catherine Parr had fallen into early labor, and unfortunately had died, along with her child.

The Princess' world soured, even more by the fact that Edward expected her to be back soon.

Days later, Elizabeth was still mourning, moody and tired of the numerous condolences the French royals bestowed her. Soon, another letter arrived, and Elizabeth could not help but be tense as she sought to open it. She could not control the laughter that left her at Kat's - her Governess' insistence that she should draft a letter to console a heartbroken Thomas in his sorrow... Sorrow? She could swear that Thomas Seymour felt no sorrow at his wife's death, and quickly wrote just that in her reply.

CHAPTER 4

After years of growing up in England as a royal, Princess Elizabeth had grown accustomed to being followed everywhere by guards. Also, she had grown accustomed to being gossiped about by the court. But ever since she had arrived from France, the courtiers and nobles had done none of that. She had expected that, though it still took her off guard. They had witnessed the shaming Elizabeth could dish out. Not long after she had left for France, King Henry had ordered some courtiers stripped to their undergarments and whipped unconscious for such murmurings.

She walked through the corridors of the Castle, her spine straight, her manner poised. She made it past the courtiers and the silence was deafening. Soon she arrived at her chambers' doors and left the guards beyond. What she did not expect, however, was a furious man in a black tunic at her back - Thomas Seymour.

He gripped her arm and pulled her toward him, a hand closing over her mouth. Before he could do anymore, Elizabeth had a dagger on his neck and a wild taunting grin on her face.

Try it, she teased. Her hand was steady and her mind accepting, the cruel fact that she would tear his neck open if he made a wrong move. With a nervous chuckle he pulled back, his intentions having failed; she could see his rage now.

The Princess tightened her grip on the dagger. She found herself insulted by how easily he had hoped to catch her off guard. They were both standing just outside her door. The hallway beyond was quiet and uncrowded. Thomas knew that a slight scream from her would have the guards rushing in.

She clicked her tongue at him and moved to sit on an armchair in the hosting room they were in. Ever watching him, his head shifted in her direction. Elizabeth flashed him a grin. He looked forward again, his fist tightening in rage. What a shame!!!

It was flattering, she supposed, how he still felt the need to try and dominate her. How he still thought her a frightened little girl. She smirked at him and waited patiently for him to find a word.

At last, his face had finally decided to settle on a hue between the red-and-purple of thick embarrassment and fury. Lord Thomas deflated into a chair opposite her.

"I see you are out of mourning." She mocked, nonplussed by the flashy colors he wore.

He clenched his jaw for so long, that she was stunned when she heard no cracking. Then, after some obvious consideration, he dragged his chair closer to Elizabeth, careful to stay out of the reach of her dagger. "You would rather remain forever in your brother and sister's mercy?" he asked, sounding faintly amused.

"If I truly believed the honesty in your questions, your oh so touching care, I wouldn't feel so inclined to laugh."

"You will believe me, if you give me a chance to show you how much I care about you." His palms were sweaty as he gripped her free hand, the one without the knife, his attempt at vulnerability. *A new playing tactic this time?*

The doors groaned open to reveal a stunned maid. The glass of cider in her hand slipped to the floor and shattered in a surprisingly loud crescendo. She screamed and a guard came promptly, peeking through the open door. He froze at the sight of Thomas, before hurrying inside, hand on the hilt of his sword, drawing it free.

"We are fine in here," Elizabeth laughed and waved him away. She asked that he help the maid clear the glass shards laid strewn. The guard growled, looking as if he might refuse, but instead bowed slightly at Elizabeth's glare and did as he was told. He left the room with the maid and shut the door on their way out.

"They recognize you still, how, pray, tell? stepfather does that make you feel?"

"I want the best for you."

"I don't quite comprehend how your actions tally."

"I..." he started, glancing around before leaning into her, "I wish you to be Queen, your Majesty."

Elizabeth's eyes narrowed and she pulled away from him, slipping out of the chair and she began pacing, a thousand thoughts running through her mind, "That's treason Lord Seymour."

"Is it? Edward should not even be King, he—

"He is and nothing short of death will change that!"

"My point exactly," he said a manic grin in his eyes as he stood and walked towards her, "You deserve the world my Love, let me put you on your throne. It is your birthright."

Elizabeth looked at him, really looked and shook her head in pity and utter disgust. She raised her dagger pointing towards the door, "Your offer is not appreciated. Get out before I have my guards arrest you for treason."

"Elizabeth listen—

"Listen here, you swine!" she yelled, rushing at him, and pressed her dagger against his neck. She delighted in the frightened swallow he made. "I see your true intentions and I am no puppet for you to play. You do not want a Queen; you wish that through me you will be King. Now leave before I pare you myself."

She shoved him away from her and retreated into her bedroom, shaking with rage and disgust. Whatever he planned; he would not accomplish it through her. She was no one's puppet. She would not be manipulated.

England 1939

Elizabeth lay on her back, surveying the small room where she had been brought. The gloomy sky outside the tower is doing little to brighten space. Despite what Mary had said to mock her, she knew for certain this was not her death place. She had heard of the fact that this was the tower her mother had been brought to before her execution. Elizabeth was certain that her death was most certainly not going to be here.

The coarse mattress beneath her smelled of dried sweat and urine. Elizabeth tried not to think about what had caused the ring of stains marring the surface; or the prisoners that had laid on it or the ages since it had been in use. The tower room was chilly and drafty, with several bricks broken and missing from the walls. A numbing breeze blew through the cramped space. Elizabeth shivered; her dress still damp from the rain the guards had dragged her in from. She pulled at the ropes that secured her cold hands and feet, hissing as a sharp pain pierced her side. The two guards had been far from gentle since she had struggled. She had waited for Edward to explain the reason for her arrest before roaring with rage. The guards had knocked her to the ground. Elizabeth was sure she had cracked a rib when she landed. There had to be some way out of this mess. She hoped the evidence from her guards and maids would be enough this time.

If only she had decided to report the fool, Thomas Seymour. He had been in her chambers with his treasonous words. Would they have believed her? If she had, none of this would have happened. Thomas Seymour would not have continued with his plans of conspiring to depose Somerset as the Protector of the crown and marrying Lady Jane Grey - a cousin of theirs to Edward.

His plans were to take Elizabeth as his own wife and rid himself of the King, to become King himself.

Now, his actions had raised suspicions against her. Mary did not think twice before advising Edward to have her evicted from her rooms and to be imprisoned in the tower.

But for how long? Edward had said that he intended for her to remain there for the duration of the investigation. What if? What if he decided to kill her? What if he favored Mary's prejudices against her?

It was late in the evening, and she had been here for hours. The Kingdom would have heard of her arrest by now. They would be humming their mockery of her. Would Edward decide against her? Would... She squeezed her eyes shut against the prickle of tears. It was no use getting upset over what has happened. Right now, she needed to concentrate and gather strength for when the investigator would arrive. She needed composure and strength. She would not be dragged into her death. Not when she was innocent.

The door opened, and they entered, their silhouette illuminated by the candle in the hallway. The investigator walked in alongside some guards. It was time for her questioning. Mary might have influenced him, but she would be no fool.

The guards came to her and untied her bound limbs before retreating. Elizabeth stood up slowly, calmly and watched him assess her. She remained unflinching, not breaking into the sob that tickled the roof of her mouth or pleading her innocence with him.

"Why don't you take a seat," said the investigator, his spectacled gray eyes searching the gloomy interior.

Elizabeth shrugged, moving to the chair that many before her had seated and watched the man that might decide her fate slip into the chair across from her. He was quite unremarkable for the role he might play.

"I'm not guilty." Her voice was steady, her manner - poised.

He shook his head slightly as he opened his documents. "It will not do you any good to talk unless I bid you. You will need all your effort when I commence shortly."

Elizabeth held out her hands. "At least have the guards fetch me a tumbler of water."

"I will be done with you soon. Tell me, why do you seek to clear your path to the throne."

"Lord Seymour told you that?" Lest he suspects informality.

"Don't divert my questions."

"Your facts are muffled investigator, I'm not an accomplice."

"Then why didn't Thomas Seymour list you as one?"

"He didn't," she replied, smiling at the investigator's stunned eyebrow arch. "Because I am not an accomplice, tell me have you asked my maids, and guards, they would be willing to set you straight."

"You shall teach me how to do my job now?"

A bitter smile crossed Elizabeth's lip. Part of her longed to fly into a rage, but she knew it would not help her cause any. It would be much better to retain her wits and calm as a way out of the situation.

"A mere suggestion, I would hate for sloppiness to get me killed."

He looked stunned, albeit appalled by Elizabeth's guts, "It is very kind of My King and Princess Mary to grant you the benefit of a doubt."

"Generosity befits a King."

They launched in a back-and-forth tirade of questions, answers, and satire, until Elizabeth grew bored of his repetition. She stood abruptly from the chair.

The investigator could do nothing but watch her as she laid back onto her despicable mattress. She tuned him out, closing her eyes to the physical discomfort she felt. The bed was hellish.

Elizabeth shut her eyes and decided that she needed to conserve her strength if they decided to kill her no matter what she said. She would need the strength to make a speech at her beheading, if she were judged guilty...

A week later she was deemed innocent and freed and to her astonishment she discovered she had garnered quite the supporters - political and otherwise.

A few months later, Thomas Seymour was beheaded.

CHAPTER 5

P*RINCESS ELIZABETH*
England July 1553

She bucked, pushing her hips up to deepen his touch. Everything - his touch, his smell, his passion - was overwhelming. It was all for her. Every muscle in her stomach contracted in tune with his fingers as they slid in and out of her.

His mouth switched breasts and then lifted them one nipple at a time. He pulled himself up so that he was kissing her lips harder than ever before, passionate, and promising. His mouth slipped below her left ear and started nibbling and sucking.

"Please, Robert, please." She whispered harshly.

"Please what?"

"I do not know. Just please."

Her neck was the most sensitive part of her body. The evening stubble that peppered his jawline was sending a wildfire of sensations to her brain. He chuckled against her skin and nipped playfully along her jaw.

Each kiss had her thighs getting warmer, wetter, and so much wilder!

She wrapped her hand around his member and stroked him a few times. He hooked his arm under her knee and lifted her leg so that she was open to him. His strong fingertips softly stroked her hardened nub. He skillfully sunk a finger deep inside her. Her legs jerked as a whimper escaped her mouth as she held onto him tighter, her nerves singing through her body. His mouth dropped onto her clitoris and slurped greedily at it. He then focused back to her breast, a teasing smile on his face while his fingers continued their assault. First just one finger, and then two, repeatedly. The sensation was explosive.

"R-Robert—" She gasped, feeling her body starting to lock up. "I am quite near."

He did not stop but sped up, driving her body higher until she exploded into ecstasy.

Her body was still quaking, his fingers still stroking, in and out of her slowly. He gasped in a rugged low as she wrapped her fingers around his member in admiration. It was like an aphrodisiac. He had so much heat trapped in his cock. Her mind was whirling with all the ways she could help him release it.

His cheek rubbed against hers as his teeth nibbled at her ear causing her to moan.

"My Lady," he groaned. She skillfully slid her hand up and down his cock. "I want you."

Before she could say a word, he swiftly mounted atop her. His hands squeezed her hips, holding her down as if he thought she would change her mind. She doubted she could if she wanted to.

His fingers shook as he rested above her, hoisting himself on his elbows. She held her breath and waited until he was well positioned between her legs. She then guided his cock to her entrance, sheathing him in her warmth.

He sank into her in one fluid motion. "Dear Lord." His words were a cross between a moan and a groan.

Her back arched and her mouth let out a guttural gasp as he stilled deep within her.

"Elizabeth," Robert panted, his muscles straining as he held himself back until she adjusted to his size.

He moved slowly at first before picking up his pace. She pushed up wantonly to meet each thrust as he pounded into her. Grabbing her leg, he lifted it, stretching her so that it was over her head. He was deep, deeper than she had ever imagined. His rhythm was fluid and hard, so delightfully perfect. She tilted her hips and tried to meet his thrusts, the need inside her begging for release. It was all she could do to hold back, because she did not want this to end so soon.

Robert was not willing to let her keep what bit of control she was so desperately holding on to. His ardent thrusts turned slow but deep as he rocked against her. The sensation was of him rubbing against her clitoris with delicious pressure.

"FFFFFFFFFFFFFuck—"

She reached up and their mouths melded together as her vision blurred under the onslaught of pleasure.

"God, you are so beautiful." He did not stop as her body clenched tighter around him. Her heart felt like it was trying to hammer its way out of her chest. The more he moved inside her, the longer her orgasm stretched. She was ready to beg him to stop.

Then, like a flick of a switch, his thrusts turned to brutal poundings. She could feel his cock throbbing. Her hands slipped along his sweat-drenched shoulders, and she wrapped her legs around his waist, pulling him deeper into her. Her body quivered as his cock pulsed inside her causing her to scream. He called her name mingled-in with suggestive curses, as his muscles stiffened, his eyelids squeezed shut. They both shattered into subliminal ecstasy.

They barely rested, before they fell upon themselves again. They drove each other in a heady numbness, over and over, carnal nuances echoing throughout the private room.

Hours later while he slept in the bed, his arm tightly wrapped around her. Princess Elizabeth managed to slip out of his arms and bed, proceeding to shuffle into her cloth. Her steps were furtive as she slithered through the secret corridor, free of courtiers, maids, or guards, back to her room. Almost immediately, a guard rapped at her door with an announcement - King Edward VI had died. The tuberculosis had finally claimed him.

As she rushed out of the door, she could not help the tears that slipped unbridled from her eyes.

She had a heart wrenching pain in her heart. Her baby brother was now dead!

England 1553

The tremors of a royal death at times builds in crescendo, like a war.

Edward had died but left behind a royal mess. He had ignored the Act of succession and had excluded both Mary and Elizabeth from succeeding him. In his will, their cousin Lady Jane Grey, had been named the heir to the throne. This left a smarting insult to Mary and Elizabeth.

Mary was both furious and slighted. She had made it a point not to take this news quietly. She quickly summoned her supporters and had a meeting with Elizabeth. Both had come to terms with the fact that they had to recover the throne.

On the third day of August that year, Mary rode into the castle with Elizabeth at her side. Without much ado, they were triumphant in their cause. Soon after Mary was crowned Queen.

Mary was now Queen. The unity that Elizabeth had established with her years ago was now long gone. Years of hate and a clash of opinions had eroded what was once a unified front between them.

Mary proceeded to rule England. Her reign claimed the lives of numerous reformists and protestants. It also won her the title - Bloody Mary. She proved to be much more brutal than her father had been.

Elizabeth had to patiently play smart in those tumultuous times. She practiced her faith privately and yet outwardly agreed with everything Mary did. Queen Mary had even insisted that every Citizen of England attend mandatory Catholic service only as a rule.

Time went on as blood flowed rampantly - a blood tyrant she was.

Soon discontent spread rapidly through the country. Many, to her great shock, looked to Elizabeth as a focus for their opposition to Mary's tyranny and religious policies.

In 1554 a rebellion grew that sought to overthrow Queen Mary. However, this revolt was suppressed, and all suspects were interrogated, Elizabeth included. Elizabeth found herself once more fighting to prove her innocence. She had in no way been part of this plot against her sister.

There were much dallying and numerous consultations by Mary's advisors on whether to kill Elizabeth. The pressure on Mary from Elizabeth's supporters was too much. She could not kill her without concrete proof. She opted then to place herself on house arrest, for a year.

In 1555, Elizabeth was called before court to be with Mary in the last stages of her pregnancy with King Phillip - her husband. If the child was born successfully, then Elizabeth would never be Queen.

As fate would have it, the child did not survive. It was now clear to all but Mary, that after the queen's death, Elizabeth would rule.

November, that same year, Mary gave in and acknowledged Elizabeth as her heir. In 1558 she too died, leaving Elizabeth as her successor.

England January 1559

The deafening roar of the crowd echoed as she walked through them to the pale stone corridors of Westminster Abbey, London. They were chanting her name, almost wailing it. Queen Elizabeth!!!

Her heart thudded with pride as they clapped - a two-beat pulse that sounded through each step she took along the crowded corridor. The orb and the cross were an assuring weight in her hands. The ornate rubies that decorated them smoldered in the light of the sun trickling from the landing above. Her gown was beautiful yet simple. Its numerous folds swirled with elegant designs and her face was caked in royal splendor, composed and ever beautiful.

She reached the landing and climbed up into the building. She went past the towering, muscled guards who lurked in the shadows just beyond the open archway. Her guards. Her council.

Robert was there, and a few others whose faces were obscured by the shadows. Their faces stretched gleefully as they gave her cheerful grins. This moment would be carefully etched into history. Everything was about to change.

The chanting increased, and the locket she wore bounced between her breasts with each step. Her mother's locket - Anne

Boleyn's locket. She kept her eyes ahead, a full smile on her face as she emerged at last onto the open roofed podium. The elated cries of her supporters grew frantic, as overpowering as the frenzied crowd outside the abbey. In the streets, hundreds gathered and were chanting her name. In the corner, young musicians of apt skill played in harmony to each pulse of the claps. A staggeringly beautiful sight.

Hallowed was this power and the crown she had attained, what she had endured to get it. What she meant for her supporters, opened the opportunity to usher in the Protestant religion firmly. Elizabeth was a light after the shadows of Mary's bloody rule. This moment had been nothing short of a dream for them. But now that she was Queen, they seemed much more achievable.

"Queen Elizabeth Daughter of Anne Boleyn.
Beloved.
Virtuous.
Blessed.
Elizabeth of England.
The Beauty of England.
Elizabeth the new dawn."!!!!

She cleared her throat, her heart warmer than ever. She waited for their silence.

"I thank the Lord and you all. I am here concerning your request that I should continue to remain a good Lady and Queen. Be assured that I will be as good unto you as any Queen was unto her people. I pledge that with every will in me, and every power I have. Know here today, that for the safety and peace of you all, I will not hesitate, if there is need, to spend my blood. God thank you all."

She blinked back tears as their cheers sent rippling tremors through the entirety of Westminster Abbey. She smiled at the crowd, at her people, at her world, so ready and ripe for the taking.

Yet this was not the end - this was not her end. She had survived loss, pain, and torture. As well, she had survived molestation, hatred, and despair. Whatever may come she would survive it too. Hers was not a story of weakness. She was not afraid of what may come. She had faith in the Lord leading and holding her. She had the full support of the countrymen and council. As much as she had faith in herself.

The Queen nodded and moved back into the hall, delighted while entertaining her guests. Somewhere dep down in her bloodline, she felt an embrace; one so warm as her mother's touch.

Finally, it now seemed that Queen Elizabeth, daughter of Anne Boleyn, last surviving heir of King Henry VIII had a hopeful future.

The END

ABOUT THE AUTHOR

Ava Axton is a bestselling author of action-adventure romance novels, known for her ability to captivate readers with heart and soul.

With a colorful life that includes being a wife, mother, former gymnast, actress, musician, and charity voice, Ava finds inspiration in remote resorts and camping trips.

Her stories transport readers to lush, untamed lands where brave, flawed heroes and strong, independent women exist in a world where chivalry still thrives.

Ava's captivating writing style continues to win the hearts of millions worldwide, making her books a must-read for romance fans.

Additional Author Books

- **Paramour King**[1]

- **Maverick Crown**[2]

- **Long Live the Queen**[3]

- **Butterfly Rising**[4]

---

1. https://www.amazon.com/dp/B09RSS9XLB

2. https://www.amazon.com/dp/B09SXW1FMQ

3. https://www.amazon.com/dp/B09SY25RM4

4. https://www.amazon.com/dp/B09SXVDQBF

<u>Leave Me a Review!</u>

If you really enjoyed this book or found it useful, please take a moment to leave a review on Amazon.

I'm interested in learning what you like, think, and want. I read all the reviews personally.

https://www.amazon.com/dp/B09SXVDQBF

Thank you so much for your support!

Don't miss out!

Visit the website below and you can sign up to receive emails whenever Ava Axton publishes a new book. There's no charge and no obligation.

https://books2read.com/r/B-A-EYOR-CZGJC

BOOKS 2 READ

Connecting independent readers to independent writers.

Did you love *Butterfly Rising*? Then you should read *Colossus Unravelling* by Ava Axton!

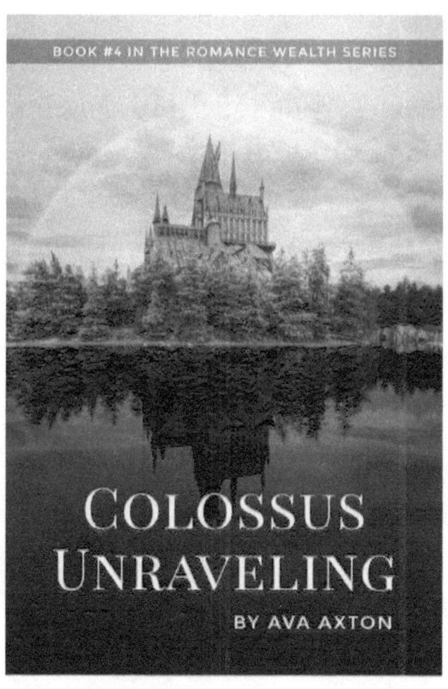

An engaging fictionalized account of the 16th century King of England, Henry VIII's romance with Anne Boleyn dubbed "the King's great matter".

It explores the events of the life and death of the infamous Anne Boleyn and the passion and tragedy brought by her marriage to King Henry VIII.

When Anne failed to bear a male heir, the King set his sights outside their marriage. And the Boleyn family faced their repercussions - the death of Anne and her brother George and ghastly shame to their name.

Anne's blood has barely dried and now the King sits on his throne, a new bride beside him.

His passion as now as fierce as his hate, his heart blacker than the inkiest depths.

Now done with the pretense of any interest in his female heirs, he begins a quest from Queen to Queen, his only interest lying in power, women, and an heir.

But Karma possesses inhuman patience.

And so, despite his obsessions granting him a son and power and more women, it gifts him a disease and a new title - the King of delirium.

Read more at https://www.amazon.com/author/avaaxton.

Also by Ava Axton

Romance Wealth Series
Butterfly Rising

Watch for more at https://www.amazon.com/author/avaaxton.

# About the Author

Ava Axton is a bestselling author of action-adventure romance novels, known for her ability to captivate readers with heart and soul.

With a colorful life that includes being a wife, mother, former gymnast, actress, musician, and charity voice, Ava finds inspiration in remote resorts and camping trips.

Her stories transport readers to lush, untamed lands where brave, flawed heroes and strong, independent women exist in a world where chivalry still thrives.

Ava's captivating writing style continues to win the hearts of millions worldwide, making her books a must-read for romance fans.

Read more at https://www.amazon.com/author/avaaxton.

9 798223 052241